Dear Parents:

Congratulations! Your child is taking the first steps on an exciting journey. The destination? Independent reading!

STEP INTO READING® will help your child get there. The program offers five steps to reading success. Each step includes fun stories and colorful art or photographs. In addition to original fiction and books with favorite characters, there are Step into Reading Non-Fiction Readers, Phonics Readers and Boxed Sets, Sticker Readers, and Comic Readers—a complete literacy program with something to interest every child.

Learning to Read, Step by Step!

Ready to Read   Preschool–Kindergarten
• big type and easy words • rhyme and rhythm • picture clues
For children who know the alphabet and are eager to begin reading.

Reading with Help   Preschool–Grade 1
• basic vocabulary • short sentences • simple stories
For children who recognize familiar words and sound out new words with help.

Reading on Your Own   Grades 1–3
• engaging characters • easy-to-follow plots • popular topics
For children who are ready to read on their own.

Reading Paragraphs   Grades 2–3
• challenging vocabulary • short paragraphs • exciting stories
For newly independent readers who read simple sentences with confidence.

Ready for Chapters   Grades 2–4
• chapters • longer paragraphs • full-color art
For children who want to take the plunge into chapter books but still like colorful pictures.

STEP INTO READING® is designed to give every child a successful reading experience. The grade levels are only guides; children will progress through the steps at their own speed, developing confidence in their reading.

Remember, a lifetime love of reading starts with a single step!

For Lisah
—P.B.

Visit us on the Web!
StepIntoReading.com
rhcbooks.com

Educators and librarians, for a variety of teaching tools, visit us at
RHTeachersLibrarians.com

ISBN 978-0-7364-3182-8 (trade) — ISBN 978-0-7364-8157-1 (lib. bdg.)
ISBN 978-0-7364-3183-5 (ebook)

Printed in the United States of America   10 9 8 7 6 5 4 3 2 1

Disney

101 DALMATIANS

adapted by Pamela Bobowicz

illustrated by the Disney Storybook Art Team

Random House 🏠 New York

Pongo is a dog.

Roger is a man.

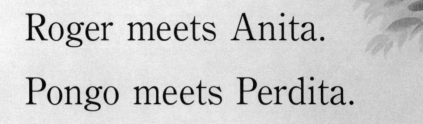

Roger meets Anita.

Pongo meets Perdita.

Nanny takes care.

Puppies are here!

Puppies grow.

They watch a show.

Puppies sleep tight.

Puppies go missing
one night!

Bark, bark!

All-dog alert!

Friends help search.

Puppies wait to be found.

Evil Cruella is around!

The cat
leads the pack.

Pongo and Perdita attack!

Now they have <u>more</u> puppies!

Time to hide.

Roll and slide.

Quick, quick, quick!
Cruella is tricked.

Puppies are home,
safe and sound.

The big, big family
gathers around.